FLO
The Lyin' Fly

Also Available

Board Books:
Hermie: A Common Caterpillar
Flood of Lies
Hermie and the Big Bully Croaker
Rock, Roll, and Run
Stuck in a Stinky Den
The Caterpillars of Ha-Ha

Picture Books:
Hermie: A Common Caterpillar
Flo the Lyin' Fly

Videos & DVDs:
Hermie: A Common Caterpillar
Flo the Lyin' Fly

MAX LUCADO'S

Hermie & Friends

FLO
The Lyin' Fly

MAX LUCADO

Story by Troy Schmidt

Illustrations by GlueWorks Animation

Based on the characters from Max Lucado's
Hermie: A Common Caterpillar

Tommy
NELSON

A Division of Thomas Nelson, Inc.

www.hermieandfriends.com
Email us at: comments@hermieandfriends.com

Don't use your mouth to tell lies.
Don't ever say things that are not true.

—Proverbs 4:24 ICB

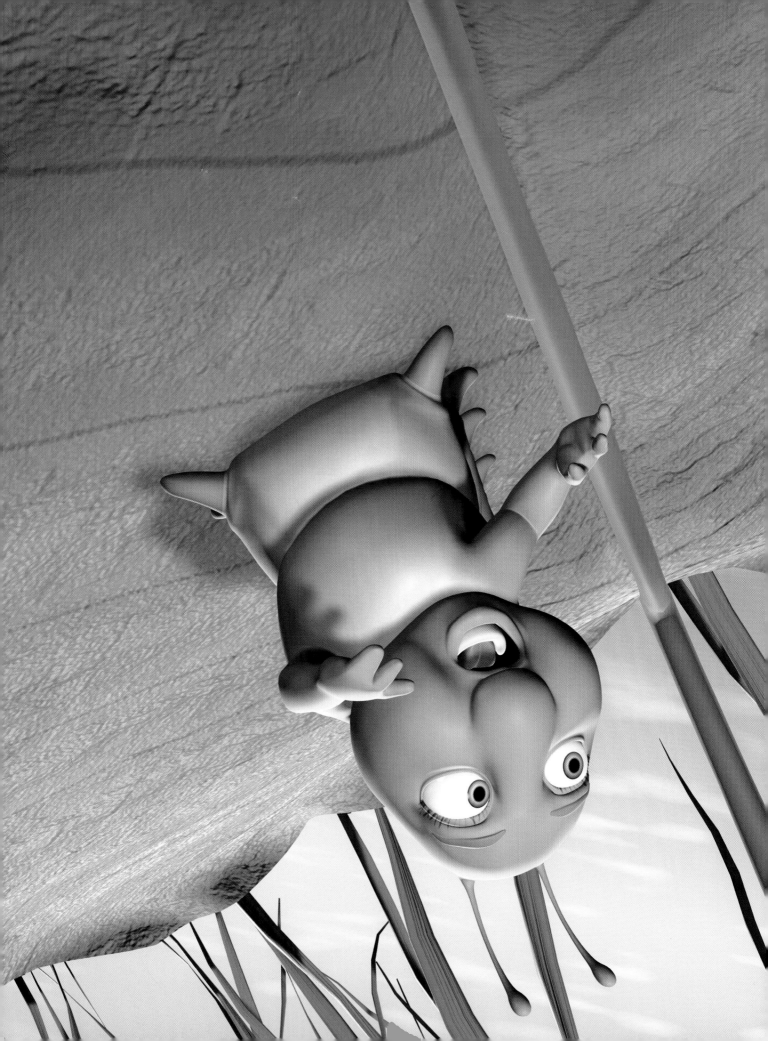

Hermie the caterpillar and his best friend, Wormie, were sound asleep. Suddenly, they were awakened by a scream.

"Heeeellllpppp!"

Startled, Hermie and Wormie fell from their upside-down beds right on their heads.

"Heeeelllpppp!" There it was again.

Someone was in trouble. Hermie and Wormie rushed to help.

It was Flo the fly.

"What is it? What's wrong?" Hermie asked as he tried to catch his breath.

"You should see the looks on your faces!" Flo said as she burst into laughter. "Nothing was wrong. I was just having a little fun."

Hermie and Wormie crawled off. They weren't having fun. Flo's trick had made them angry.

The next day, the ladybug twins, Hailey and Bailey, were listening to one of Flo's awesome adventures. They didn't know her stories were all lies.

In this story, Flo battled a fierce dragonfly with just a pine-needle sword and a leaf shield. She told of the dragonfly's hot, fiery breath (dragonflies don't have hot, fiery breath), and how she rode on the dragonfly's back (of course, this never happened, either). And how . . .

Just then, Hermie and Wormie came by and heard Flo's lie.

"Story time is over!" Hermie said. Then he and Wormie sent the twins home.

"Why'd you do that?" Flo whined. "I was just having some fun."

"It was a lie," said Wormie. "Just like last night when you made us think you were in trouble."

"But the dragonfly story wasn't *all* a lie. I saw a dragonfly . . . once. It flew right over my head."

Hermie sighed. "But it's a lie because you said it is true, and it is *not* true."

But Flo didn't care. She flapped her wings and off she flew.

Hermie prayed, "God, please help Flo tell the truth. She does so many good things, but when she lies we can't trust her."

"Ahhhhhhhhhhhhh!" Flo screamed.

Once again, Hermie and Wormie ran up, out of breath. "What is it? What's wrong?" they shouted.

"Look!" Flo pointed at a poster. "The Water Beetles are coming. They are my favorite band of all time. Stringo, Lingo, Bingo, and Zingo!"

"Ahhhhhhhhhhhhh!" screamed Annie Ant and Caitlin Caterpillar, and Hailey, Bailey, and Lucy Ladybug as they crowded around the poster. "The Water Beetles in concert . . . here . . . tomorrow!"

Everyone turned to Flo. Her friends thought she knew lots of famous people, but she didn't. Those were all lies she had told.

"Hey, Flo, do you know the Water Beetles?" Hailey asked.

Before Flo knew it, she heard herself saying, "Sure I do. In fact, we're best friends."

The girls couldn't believe it. Hermie and Wormie couldn't believe it. No one could believe it. Even Flo herself couldn't believe she'd said it.

"Please, please, please, introduce us to them!" the girls all begged.

"Okay, be at my house tomorrow morning," Flo said as she walked away. Flo didn't know what she was going to do. She didn't know the Water Beetles. Then she got an idea.

When the girls showed up, Flo pointed to a field. In the shadows stood four figures, who . . . looked . . . a little . . . like the Water Beetles.

Just then one of the Beetles fell down. "Stay here!" yelled Flo. But it was too late.

Annie ran to help. "Hey! These are just sticks and acorns made to look like the Water Beetles!"

Bailey pointed at Flo. "You don't know the Water Beetles! You lied!"

Caitlin Caterpillar led the group away. "C'mon, girls, I'm not listening to these lies anymore."

Flo's friends were gone. She was all alone.

Flo cried and prayed. "God, are You there?"

"Always, Flo."

"My friends don't like me."

"Flo, they don't trust you because you lied," God said.

Flo looked up through her tears. "I don't want to lie anymore, but how do I tell the truth?"

"Be like Me, Flo," God said. "You can always trust Me. When I make a promise, I keep it. When I say something, I mean it. You can do the same. If you do, you will win back the trust of your friends."

"Will You help me?"

"I will," God said.

Suddenly, Flo heard a voice behind her.
"Excuse me. Can you help us?"

Flo turned around. She could not believe her eyes.
"The Water Beetles!" Flo screamed.

"We're lost," said Bingo.

"We need to get to the concert tonight," said Stringo.

"Do you know where we are?" asked Zingo.

"Can you help us?" asked Lingo.

"Yes, I can!" said Flo. "First, come to my house and have some mango nectar." This was the most exciting thing that had ever REALLY happened to Flo.

While the Water Beetles rested at Flo's, she zipped off to tell her friends the news.

First, Flo found Lucy, Hailey, and Bailey Ladybug.

"You won't believe it," Flo cried. "The Water Beetles got lost, and they're at my house."

The Ladybugs laughed out loud. Flo was right . . . they didn't believe it.

Next, Flo found Annie Ant and Caitlin Caterpillar.

"Stringo, Lingo, Bingo, and Zingo are staying with me until the concert tonight! You want to meet them?"

Annie and Caitlin covered their ears and hummed. They didn't want to hear any more of Flo's lies.

Finally, Flo found Hermie and Wormie.

"I really met them. I'm telling the truth!"

Hermie and Wormie said nothing. They were sad for Flo the fly and all her lies.

"Nobody believes me. The most exciting thing has just happened, and nobody believes me. It's all because of the lies I told." Flo flew off.

What Flo didn't know was that someone
was watching her. Someone very mysterious.
And he believed her story.

When Flo got back, Stringo asked, "Hey, what do you do for fun around here?"

Flo took them petal diving, pond swimming, daisy sledding, and clog dancing. They even spent some time riding roller coasters and Ferris wheels. For Flo, it had been a perfect day with her favorite singing group. Sadly, she knew no one would believe her.

"This is fun!" said Stringo.

"But haven't we forgotten something?" asked Zingo.

"The concert!" cried Bingo.

"We're late," yelled Lingo.

"C'mon, I'll show you the way," Flo said as she led them into the foggy marsh.

It was night. Spooky sounds filled the air.

Unknown to Flo and the Water Beetles, someone was watching them, lurking in the shadows. Someone big and scary.

Out of the darkness flew a dangerous dragonfly. He scooped up the Water Beetles and took them to his home at the top of a tree.

"Oh, no! Heeeellpppp! Heeeellpppp!" Flo screamed. But no one came.

Quickly, Flo hurried to the concert, rushed onto the stage, and grabbed the microphone. Standing before all the fans, she yelled, "Heeeellllpppp! Heeeellllpppp! The Water Beetles have been kidnapped!"

The crowd looked up, but no one believed her.

"Really, their lives are in danger. I was showing them a shortcut to the concert when a dragonfly swooped out of the sky and carried them away."

But no one was listening to her because of all the lies she'd told before. Flo would have to help the Water Beetles all by herself.

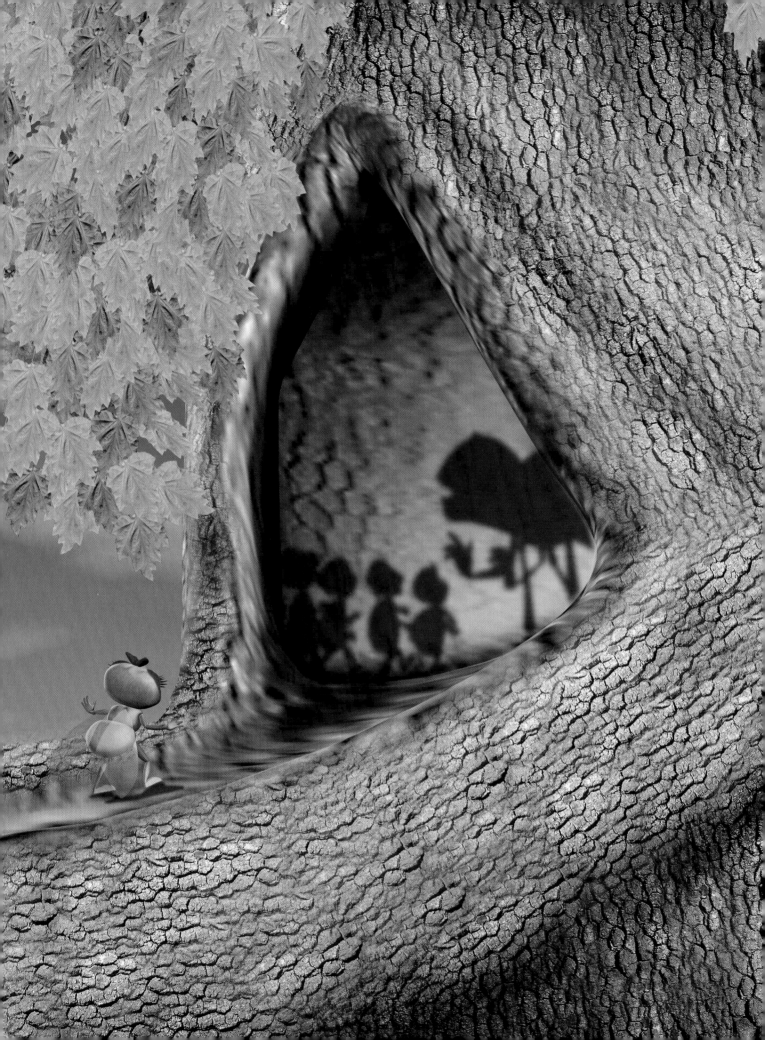

Flo flew to the dragonfly's home at the top of a
very tall tree. Then she crept softly to the door.
Her wings shaking with fear, she peeked inside.
She could see the huge shadow of the
dragonfly standing over the Water Beetles.

"Ha-ha-ha-ha-ha-ha!" chuckled the
dragonfly.

They're in danger. I have to save them.
Flo bravely stepped forward.

As Flo entered the dragonfly's home,
she couldn't believe her eyes.

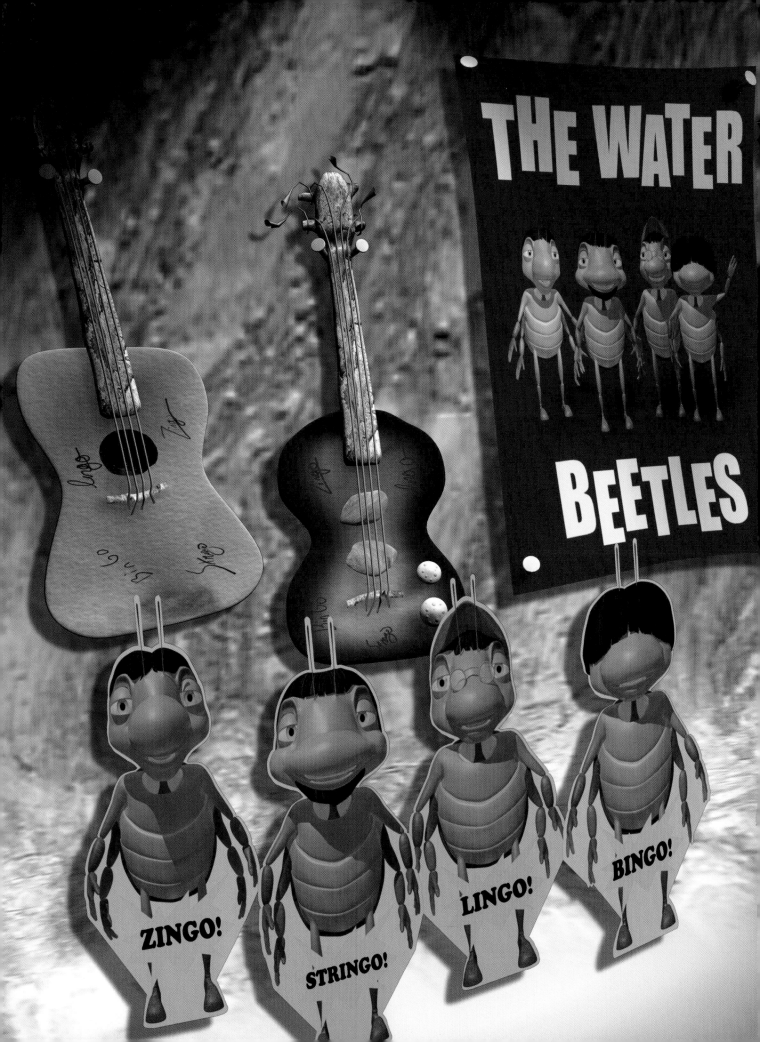

All over the walls, from the floor to the ceiling, were posters, t-shirts, hats, buttons, albums, CDs, and magazines about the Water Beetles.

"Oh, that's a good one." The dragonfly laughed at Lingo's story. Everyone giggled and slapped each other on the back.

"What's going on here?" Flo asked.

"Oh, hey, Flo," said Stringo. "This is Puffy. He couldn't get tickets to the concert and so that's why he picked us up. He wanted to meet us."

"And look at all the stuff he's collected," said Zingo.

"I am their number one fan," Puffy said, then smiled.

"That's nice." Flo smiled. "But we're late for the concert. We have to go."

"But they said they'd sing a song." Puffy frowned.

"How about we come by after the concert," Lingo replied.

Puffy glared at them and stood in their way. "I said . . . NOW!"

The Water Beetles sensed trouble. "Something tells me we should start singing." Bingo gulped.

The Water Beetles started singing their biggest hits. Puffy was so busy listening, he didn't even notice Flo tying a stick to his tail.

At just the right time, Flo yelled, "RUN!"

The Water Beetles and Flo ran out the door. Puffy followed them, but as his tail went out the door, the stick got stuck. Puffy had to stop and untie his tail.

Quickly, one by one, Flo gave Bingo, Zingo, and Lingo a ride to the bottom. But she wasn't fast enough. Puffy was loose. He zoomed after Stringo. With nothing else to do, Stringo jumped. As Stringo fell, Flo caught him and set him down with the others.

Puffy swooped down from the sky, heading straight for them. But Flo saw him coming and hurried the Water Beetles on their way.

"Follow this path to the end. It goes to the theater."

"What about you?" asked Stringo.

"I'm going to keep your number one fan busy."

Flo blasted off and landed on Puffy's back. She steered him away from the band. Puffy lost control and began to do loop-the-loops, fearsome falls, and spiral spins.

"You will not mess with my friends!" Flo yelled. The Water Beetles stopped and watched Flo and Puffy fly off into the distance, disappearing over the horizon. From far away came a faint sound. A splash. Then nothing.

Stringo, Lingo, Bingo, and Zingo made their way toward the concert, their heads hung low. Their friend was gone.

The concert crowd could hardly wait for the Water Beetles.

Finally, the lights dimmed and Stringo, Lingo, Bingo, and Zingo walked onto the stage. Everyone yelled and screamed, but the Water Beetles seemed sad and upset. Slowly the noise faded as Stringo began speaking.

"Bugs and buggettes, something terrible happened tonight. We were kidnapped." The crowd gasped.

Stringo told the whole story, just as Flo had told it.

The crowd could not believe it. Flo! She *was* telling the truth. After all those lies, all those fibs, all those twisted truths, this time Flo was right and nobody believed her—not even her best friends.

"Flo risked her life for us. We dedicate this first song to Flo."

"It's Flo," Bingo yelled and pointed to the sky. Everyone looked up.

Flo was riding on the back of a tired and dazed Puffy. The crowd applauded as Flo and Puffy landed on the stage.

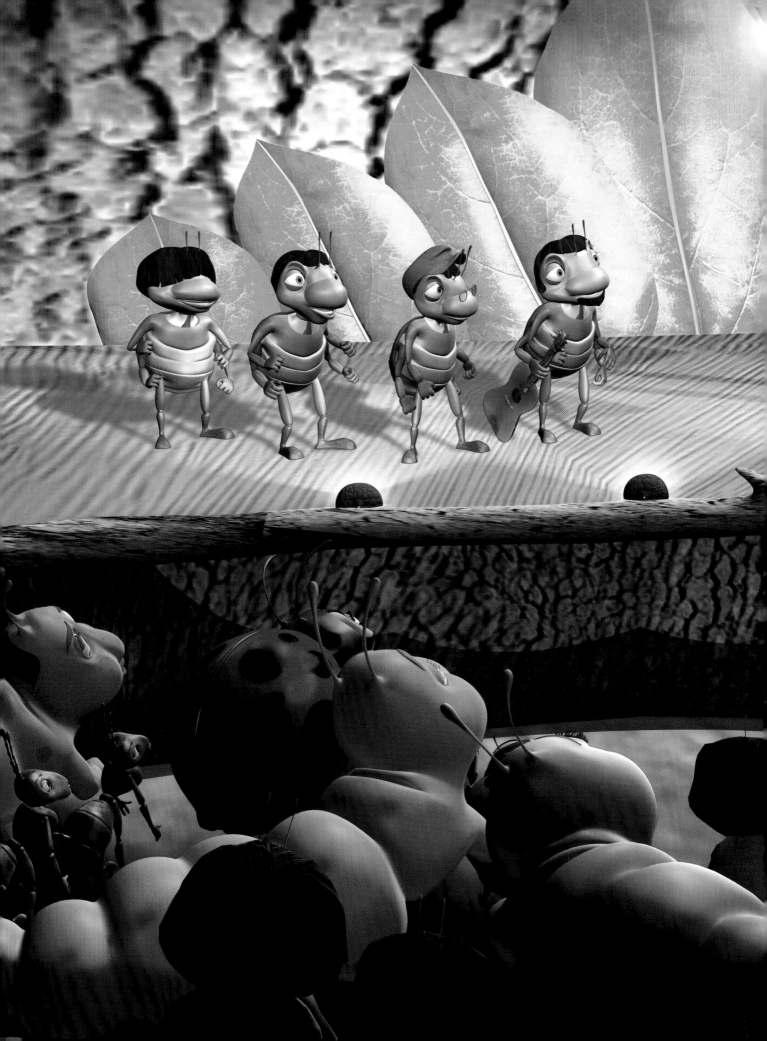

Flo faced the crowd. "I just want to apologize to everyone because of my lying. I promise that from here on, only truth will come from my mouth."

The crowd cheered. Flo had won back the trust of her friends.

In Flo's honor, the Water Beetles asked Flo to sing with them.

It was the best day of Flo's life.

"Thank You, God, for helping me learn to tell the truth."

God was proud of Flo. From now on she could be trusted. She would keep her promises. She would mean what she said. She would tell the truth.